JUSTICE HAS MANY FACES ... (Plus one extra)

SOMEWHERE, IN THE EMPTINESS OF SPACE ...

... SOMEONE IS WATCHING OVER US ...

... ENSURING THE BAD GUYS DO NOT PREVAIL.

THIS SOMEONE WAS A HERO FROM THE STARS, WHO VISITED EARTH AND DECIDED TO PROTECT OUR PLANET, MAKING IT HIS NEW HOME.

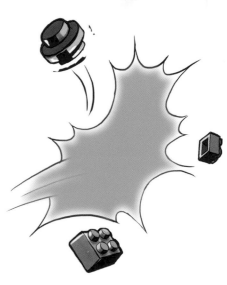

HEY, WATCH OUT!

I'M SORRY. I WAS A LITTLE DISTRACTED LISTENING TO THE STORY ABOUT THE AWESOME 'HERO FROM THE STARS'!

THEN THERE WAS GREEN LANTERN, A SPACE GUARDIAN WITH ONE OF THE MIGHTIEST WEAPONS IN THE UNIVERSE ...

THIS RING GIVES ME THE POWER TO CREATE ANYTHING!

IT CAN EVEN MAKE A QUICK IN-FLIGHT SNACK! I LOVE FRIES ... YUM!

THE FLASH – A HERO SO FAST ...

... THAT SOMETIMES HE EVEN CATCHES UP WITH HIMSELF!

?

HI!

5

WONDER WOMAN IS AN AMAZON WARRIOR WHO KNOWS NO FEAR.

I FEAR NOTHING ...

NOT EVEN THE WORLD'S WORST CRIMINALS OR THE WORLD'S HAIRIEST, GIANT SPIDERS FAZE HER!

MARTIAN MANHUNTER HAS IMMENSE POWER. HE CAN FLY, HE IS TELEPATHIC, HE CAN CHANGE HIS SHAPE AND HE CAN EVEN BECOME INVISIBLE – LIKE RIGHT NOW.

HEY! I'M NOT INVISIBLE! I'M JUST IN THE NEXT FRAME!

AND THEN THERE'S HIM ...

BATMAN – THE DARK KNIGHT! A VILLAIN'S WORST NIGHTMARE!

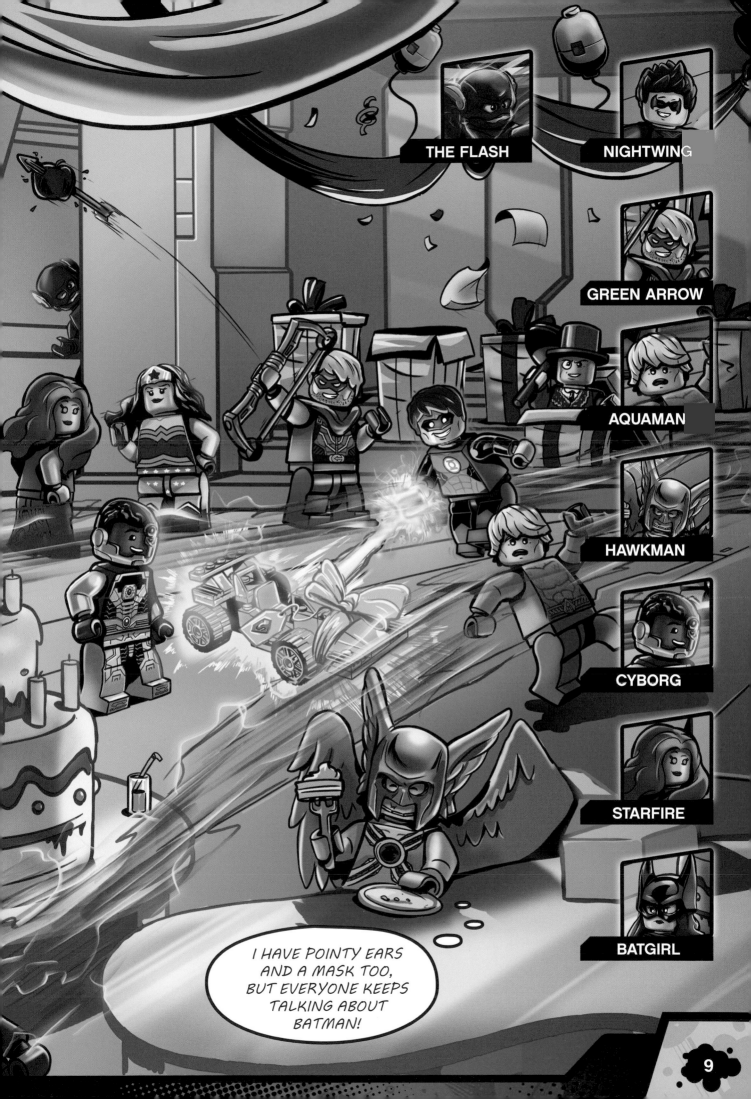

WE'RE INTERRUPTING THIS BOOK TO GIVE YOU SOME BREAKING NEWS! THERE HAS BEEN A GREAT ESCAPE FROM ARKHAM ASYLUM!

HARLEY QUINN, THE JOKER, THE PENGUIN, BRAINIAC AND POISON IVY ESCAPED BY DIGGING A TUNNEL UNDER THE ASYLUM WALL!

IT HAS BEEN REPORTED THAT THEY DUG A NUMBER OF TUNNELS, SO EITHER THEY COULDN'T LOCATE THE WALL ...

... OR THEY WERE JUST REALLY, REALLY, REALLY BORED.

GREAT ESCAPE

GCN

LIVE

Superman is flying into action to stop the escaped villains, but Batman needs to be called too. Connect the dots to make the Bat-Signal appear in the night sky.

Superman is about to enter the labyrinth of tunnels under Arkham Asylum! Help him find his way through the maze from the START to the FINISH.

START

ARKHAM ASYLUM

Once you've made it to the FINISH, turn the page to see what The Flash is up to.

FINISH

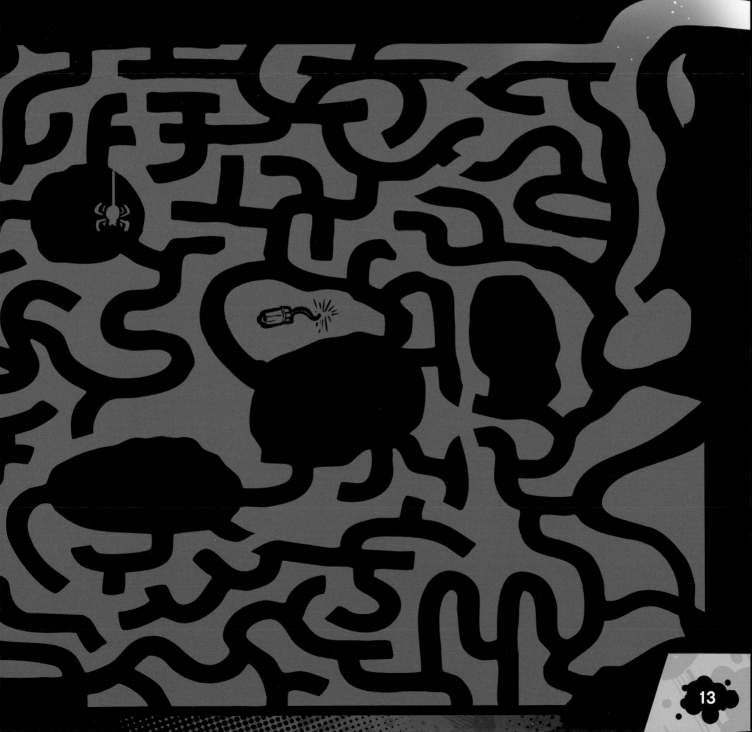

The Flash, the Fastest Man Alive, received an alarm signal. But then he got himself caught in Captain Cold's ice trap. Help him bounce off the lumps of ice by drawing lines to destroy all the snowmen in his way. The first lines have been drawn for you.

Aquaman was heading to Gotham City when he was attacked by sea creatures! It was a trap set by Black Manta, the nemesis of The King of the Seven Seas!

Which creature has entangled the watery super hero?

What's going on? Is someone trying to stop the Justice League? Turn the page to see how Batman's getting on.

Batman and Robin are pursuing the villains. The Dark Knight noticed there's something wrong with the reflection on the water. Can you spot seven differences between Gotham City and its reflection?

The escaped villains have transformed an amusement park into the Joker's Nightmare Theme Park! Spot all the fugitives in the crowd and count how many Justice League members have arrived on the scene.

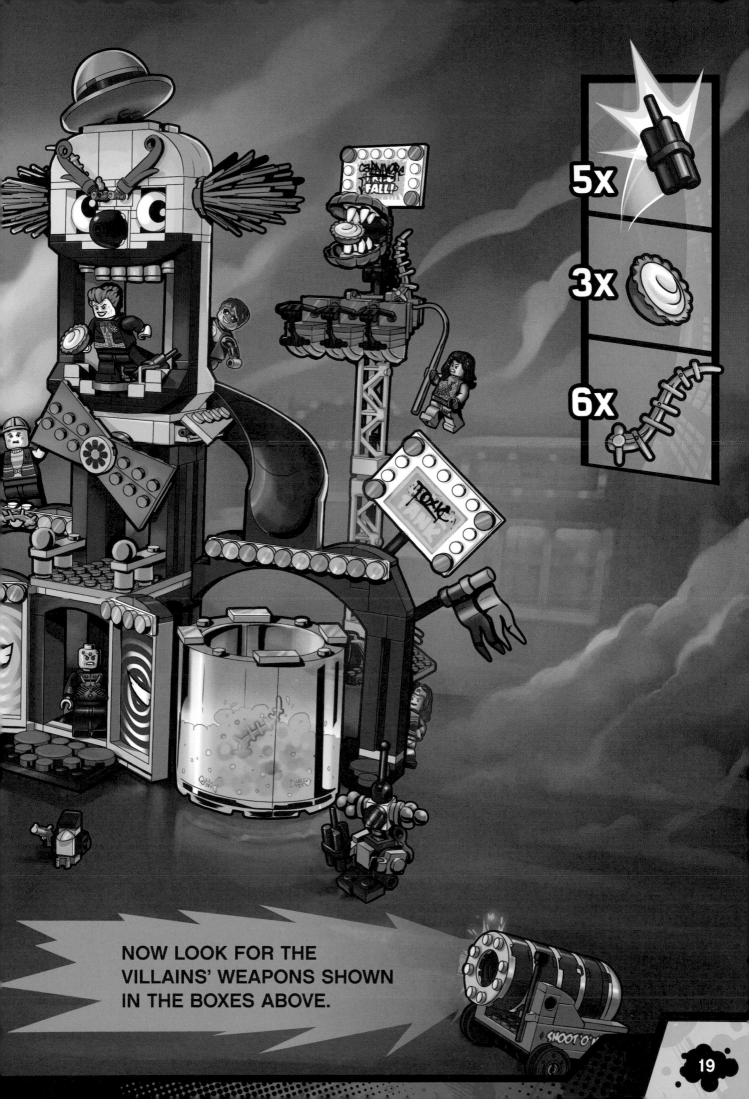

5x

3x

6x

NOW LOOK FOR THE
VILLAINS' WEAPONS SHOWN
IN THE BOXES ABOVE.

EVERY SUPER HERO HAS THEIR OWN SIGNATURE CATCHPHRASE. JUST A SIMPLE LINE OR TWO SAID BY BATMAN IS ALWAYS ENOUGH TO MAKE THE BAD GUYS' BRICKS RATTLE IN FEAR!

JUST LINES

LOOK AT ME AND IMAGINE THAT ...

... THAT ... ER, THAT ...

... WAIT A SECOND ... HOW DOES IT GO AGAIN ...

WAIT ... I KNOW I HAD A REALLY GOOD LINE TO SAY ...

IT'LL COME BACK TO ME ... ANY SECOND NOW I KNOW IT ...

CHASING BRAINIAC

DON'T LET THE SNEAKY ANDROID ESCAPE! TURN THE PAGE AND CHASE AFTER HIM WITH THE SUPER HEROES!

Brainiac fled to one of his spaceships, but which one is it? The heroes suspect the villain is hiding in the ship guarded by the most Brainiac clone-androids.

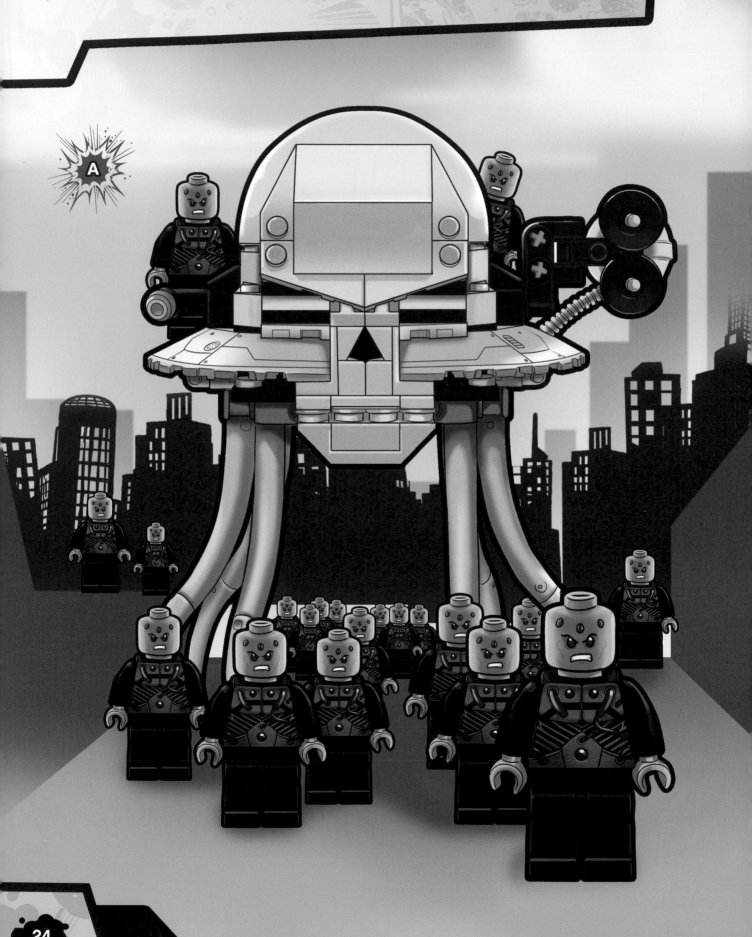

START

Brainiac has set a trap, but Superman has worked out how to beat it! See how quickly you can draw a path to Brainiac using only the pattern of coloured squares shown in Superman's thought bubble.

A WEEK IN THE LIFE OF SUPERMAN

MONDAY

Right after my morning coffee it was time for my Monday morning brawl with Darkseid in the middle of Metropolis. What better way to start the week than with some good exercise?

TUESDAY

Brainiac's androids attacked Metropolis on Tuesday! They nearly overran the whole city because it took me ages to find a free phonebox to get changed in!

On Wednesday it was Batman's birthday! I suggested that the Justice League organise a surprise party for him in the Batcave ... It turned out it wasn't the greatest idea I'd ever had.

On Thursday we had our weekly Justice League team meeting. As usual, we only discussed important things!

On Friday I destroyed a giant robot from another dimension that was threatening Metropolis. A great start to the weekend even if I do say so myself!

I decided to help Batman with his mission on Saturday. It resulted in us capturing the Joker and his gang while they were trying to rob a clown shop.

On Sunday evening I had an exclusive TV interview with the famous reporter, Lois Lane!

ANSWERS

p. 8–9

Villain: The Penguin
The Flash appears twice

p. 10–11

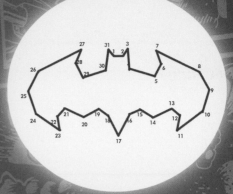

p. 12–13

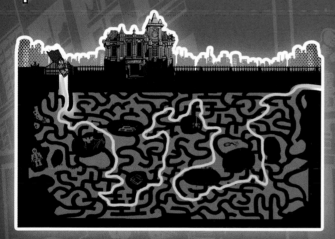

p. 14

p. 15

p. 16–17

p. 18–19

Number of Justice League Members: 6

p. 22

WHEN AQUAMAN WAS ATTACKED, I WAS AT A MIME SEMINAR.

WHEN THE FLASH WAS IN AN ICY MAZE, I WAS COOKING TOMATO SOUP.

I AM RESPONSIBLE FOR THE ESCAPE AND THE ATTACKS ON THE JUSTICE LEAGUE MEMBERS!

I HAD NOTHING TO DO WITH ANYTHING – I WAS AT THE HAIRDRESSER'S THE WHOLE TIME.

A   B   C   D

p. 26–27

FINISH

START

p. 24–25

A

p. 30

B